W9-CDO-367

ONE IS A LOT
(EXCEPT WHEN IT'S NOT)

Mượn Thị Văn

Pierre Pratt

Kids Can Press

2 is a little.

0 is nothing.

And **1** is not enough.

Except when ...

1 is a lot.

1 sun is a lot.

1 tree is a lot.

1 nut is a lot.

But **2** is too much.

1 dog is a lot.

1 squirrel is a lot.

1 bicycle is a lot.

But **O** is just right.

1 key is a lot.

1 ride is a lot.

1 leash is a lot.

But **2** is too much.

1 hello is a lot.

1 cloud is a lot.

1 umbrella is a lot.

But O is just right.

Sometimes **1** is not enough ...

And sometimes ...

1 is a lot.

For Yotam — M.T.V.

Text © 2019 Mượn Thị Văn
Illustrations © 2019 Pierre Pratt

All rights reserved. No part of this publication may be reproduced,
stored in a retrieval system or transmitted, in any form or by any means, without
the prior written permission of Kids Can Press Ltd. or, in case of photocopying
or other reprographic copying, a license from The Canadian Copyright
Licensing Agency (Access Copyright). For an Access Copyright license,
visit www.accesscopyright.ca or call toll free to 1-800-893-5777.

Kids Can Press gratefully acknowledges the financial support of the
Government of Ontario, through Ontario Creates; the Ontario Arts Council;
the Canada Council for the Arts; and the Government of Canada for
our publishing activity.

Published in Canada and the U.S. by Kids Can Press Ltd.
25 Dockside Drive, Toronto, ON M5A 0B5

Kids Can Press is a Corus Entertainment Inc. company

www.kidscanpress.com

The artwork in this book was rendered in pencil and digitally in Photoshop.
The text is set in A Pompadour.

Edited by Yasemin Uçar
Designed by Andrew Dupuis

Printed and bound in Malaysia in 3/2019 by Tien Wah Press (Pte) Ltd.

CM 19 0 9 8 7 6 5 4 3 2 1

Library and Archives Canada Cataloguing in Publication

Văn, Mượn Thị, author
One is a lot / written by Mượn Thị Văn; illustrated by Pierre Pratt.

ISBN 978-1-5253-0013-4 (hardcover)

1. Quantity (Philosophy) — Juvenile literature. 2. Number
concept — Juvenile literature. I. Pratt, Pierre, illustrator II. Title.

B105.Q34V36 2019   j119   C2018-906069-7